Contents

Chapter 1
Meet Me

Ten facts about me

1. My name is Arnold James Kean (but you can call me Arnie). I was called Arnold after my mum's favourite film star, Arnold Schwarzenegger.

2. I am 10 years, 10 months, 27 days, 4 hours, 12 minutes and 19 seconds old. Make that 20 seconds. No, 21 …

3. I am 1.5756 metres tall and weigh 44.68 kilos (before breakfast).

4. I have brown spiky hair, green eyes and a wart on my little finger. (I only found the wart this morning.)

5. I love football and my favourite team is Real Madrid.

6. I do not like green jelly because it tastes like bogeys.

7. I play for a football team called Lime Green Rovers. (My position is sub.)

8. I am in Class 6M at West Hill Primary School and my teacher is Mrs Moody-Brown. (She is a nice teacher and not moody at all.)

9. My best friend is Thomas Jones.

10. My nickname is Stat Man because I love stats, facts and figures – best of all stats about football.

****

One morning our teacher Mrs Moody-Brown asked us if we knew anything about the Greeks, because that is our class topic this term.

I put up my hand.

"Yes, Arnold?" she said.

"They won the European Football Championship in 2004, Miss," I said. "They beat Portugal 1–0 in the final."

"Arnold," Mrs Moody-Brown said with a sigh, "do you ever think about anything but football?"

"That's what my mum says," I replied. "She says I eat, sleep and dream football." (My sister Ellie says I even poo football, but that's not true.)

"Mmm, well, perhaps now you could start to eat, sleep and dream about the Ancient Greeks," said Mrs Moody-Brown.

She told us that the next day we were going to have an important visitor. His name was Dr Troy Smith and he worked in a big museum.

"He's an expert on Ancient Greece and he's coming to talk to us about it. So I want you to think of some good questions to ask him." She looked at me. "You could ask him if the Greeks played football, Arnold," she grinned. "They were very keen on sport you know. They invented the Olympic Games."

"They have football in the Olympic Games, Miss," said Thomas Jones.

"They do now, Thomas," Mrs Moody-Brown agreed, "but they didn't in ancient times. In fact they didn't have team sports at all."

She told us that at the first few Olympic Games there was only one event – a running race of about 200 metres, which was one lap around the stadium. Other events were added later – boxing, wrestling, more running races, and horse-riding. They also raced in 4-horse chariots. There was another event called the *pentathlon*. The pentathlon was made up of five events – running, long jump, wrestling, throwing the discus and the javelin.

"You know a lot about Greece, Miss," I said.

"Well, you're not the only one who likes facts, Arnold," she replied. "Now, let's see what facts you can find out about Ancient Greece before tomorrow ..."

I went on the internet as soon as I got home. The first thing I looked up was about Ancient Greece and football – and guess what? The Ancient Greeks did play a sort of football. It was called *episkyros*. It was more like rugby really because players were allowed to carry and throw the ball, as well as kick it. Most of the time there were twelve players on each side. The ball was made of linen and hair, which was wrapped in string and sewn together, so it can't have bounced much.

In a museum in Athens (that is the capital of Greece) there is a picture carved in marble which shows a Greek athlete balancing a ball on his thigh. This picture is on the European Champions' League Trophy. I told my dad this. He said the Greeks would have liked that because they loved to decorate their pots with things from their lives.

"That reminds me of a joke," he said. "What's a Grecian urn?"

"I don't know," I said.

"About 50 drachmas." Dad laughed.

"I don't get it," I said.

"It's a joke on the word *urn*, which is a kind of pot, and *earn*, as in earning money,"

Dad explained. "And drachmas are what Greek money used to be called."

I just stared at him. "I still don't get it," I said. Then I went off to see if I could find out some more about the Ancient Greeks and their sports. At least I could understand that!

My top five Ancient Olympics stats

1. Some of the Ancient Olympic events were very brutal. In one boxing match, a man called Damoxenes stuck his sharp fingernails into the body of his opponent Creugas and ripped out his guts! This broke the rules, so Creugas was named the winner even though he was dead!

2. The most violent sport in the Ancient Olympics was pankration. It was a mix of boxing and wrestling. You could do anything - kick, slap, pinch, punch - except bite or claw at your opponents' eyes, nose or mouth.

3. The hardest sport in the Games was hoplite (hoplite was the name given to foot soldiers) racing. They had to run a race in full armour and carrying heavy weapons!

4. Women were not allowed to take part in the Ancient Olympics. They couldn't even watch. But then the men had to compete with no clothes on!

5. One of the greatest sportsmen of Ancient Greece was the wrestler Milo of Kroton. He won the boys' wrestling at the Olympic Games in 540 B.C. Then he won the men's title five times from 532 to 516 B.C. He was so strong that he could tie a piece of cord round his head and then break it just by swelling up his veins!

Chapter 2
Troy's Story

The next morning Dr Troy Smith came to talk to us. I thought he would be an old man with grey hair and a grey beard and glasses, wearing a suit, like my doctor. But he wasn't. He looked about 27 years old. He had very blond hair and an earring in his left ear. He was wearing a T-shirt and jeans and red trainers. He had a nice smile. "Hi, my name's Troy Smith," he said, "and I am a museum curator. Does anyone know what a curator does?"

Katie Lee put up her hand. "No," she said.

"Oh," said Dr Troy Smith.

"Just put your hand up if you know the answer," said Mrs Moody-Brown. "Thomas?"

Thomas Jones said, "I think it's the person who looks after the objects in the museum, Miss."

Dr Troy Smith nodded. "That's right," he said. "I look after the objects from Ancient Greece. I've been interested in Ancient Greece since I was at primary school – in fact, since I was at *this* primary school." He smiled. "West Hill Primary School's where I went to school."

"Was Mrs Moody-Brown your teacher?" I asked.

Mrs Moody-Brown laughed. "I'm not that old, Arnold."

Dr Troy Smith told us that his dad was very interested in Ancient Greece too. That was why he had called his son Troy. *Troy* was the name of a very famous city in Ancient Greek myth. The Ancient Greeks fought a very long battle there.

Dr Troy Smith told us the story of the war between the Greeks and the people of Troy (who are called *Trojans*). A Trojan Prince called *Paris* ran away with *Helen*, who was the wife of *Menelaus*. He was King of the Greek state *Sparta*. The Greeks got together an army and went to the city of Troy to get Helen back. The Greeks fought the Trojans for years and years. Lots of people died on both sides, but the Greeks could not get into the city. Then one day they came up with a cunning plan. They built a huge wooden horse and hid soldiers in it. Their leader was a man called *Odysseus*. Then the rest of the army pretended to sail away, but they didn't go very far. One man called *Simon* was left behind. He told the Trojans that the horse was a gift, so they took it into their city. That night, while the Trojans were having their victory party, the Greek soldiers came out of the wooden horse. They opened the city gates and let the rest of the Greek army in. Then they killed the Trojans and burnt down their city.

"What happened to Helen?" I asked.

"She went back to Greece with Menelaus," said Dr Troy Smith. "It took seven years, though, to sail back to Greece. But it took his fellow Greek Odysseus ten years. He had lots of adventures and had to battle against many monsters, such as the huge, one-eyed *Cyclops* who ate humans."

"Cool," said Thomas Jones.

"Ancient Greece *is* cool," said Dr Troy Smith. "It's full of interesting facts and stories."

For the rest of the lesson he told us things about Ancient Greece. It was excellent. The fact I liked best was this: The Ancient Greeks worried that important secret messages might fall into their enemy's hands if they sent them in a letter, so they came up with a clever answer. They shaved the head of a messenger, wrote on his scalp and, when his hair had grown again, they sent him off. When he arrived, his hair was shaved off once more and the message read!

When Dr Troy Smith finished his talk, Mrs Moody-Brown said, "Does anyone have any questions they would like to ask our visitor?"

Katie Lee put her hand up. "Are your trainers Nike?" she asked.

Mrs Moody-Brown groaned, but Dr Troy Smith laughed.

"As a matter of fact they are," he said. "*Nike* – or Nee-kay, as we should say her name – was the Greek goddess of victory."

"And that is a very good point for me to tell you all that Dr Smith hasn't just come here to talk to us today," said Mrs Moody-Brown. "He's also come to give us exciting news about a competition."

"That's right," said Dr Troy Smith. "This term you are going to be doing projects on Ancient Greece for your topic and I am going to offer a prize for the best one. The winner will get the Troy Trophy and a £20 book token." He looked at me. "You might want to buy a new football fact book," he said with a smile.

"Or maybe a book about Ancient Greece," Mrs Moody-Brown added.

But I wasn't thinking about books or book tokens. I was thinking about how much I wanted to win that trophy!

My top five Greek life stats

1. In most of Greece only rich boys went to school and no girls did. In Sparta boys and girls went to school. But the most important lessons weren't reading and writing – they were wrestling and battle skills!

2. When a child was born in Ancient Greece, the father picked it up in his arms and danced naked around the house! But in Sparta unhealthy babies were left outside to die.

3. The Greeks ate a lot of seafood and a kind of porridge, made up of beans, lentils and corn with vegetable oil. They also ate grasshoppers! (They didn't eat jelly.)

4. The Greeks wore tunics called citons made of wool or cloth. Most families made their own clothes. They wore boots or strapped sandals. They were also the first people to wear hats with brims. The Greeks wore them when travelling and kept them on their heads with a chin strap.

5. The Greeks had pets. They liked dogs, birds, goats, tortoises and mice but they didn't keep cats.

Chapter 3
A Trip to the Museum

Mrs Moody-Brown said we should start working on our project at once. So I did. I started the day Dr Troy Smith came to our school. I went to the library and got out some books about the Greeks. I went on the internet too and found some interesting sites about Ancient Greece. My mum said she thought I should see some real Greek things, so at the weekend she took me to a museum.

We took the bus. The journey took 1 hour, 13 minutes and 47 seconds. I timed it. On the way I told Mum some of the facts I had learned about Ancient Greece, and she told me some Greek myths. She told me the story of how the hero *Perseus* killed *Medusa*.

Medusa was a *gorgon*. She had snakes for hair and if you looked in her face you got turned to stone. Perseus was clever. He held up his shield as a mirror and looked at that and not her real face. Then he chopped off her head.

Mum also told me the story of a beautiful but silly woman called *Pandora* who opened a box she was told not to open and let out all the evils and diseases of the world.

"I think Steven Morris must have been in that box," I said. Steven Morris plays for my football team, Lime Green Rovers. He is our best player, but he has a very big head and no one likes him.

"Well, hope was in the box too," Mum said. "So let's hope Steven Morris will get nicer one day."

The myth I liked best of all was about the hero *Theseus* and the *Minotaur*. The Minotaur was half-man, half-bull and lived on the Greek island of Crete in a huge underground maze called the *Labyrinth*. The Minotaur was very strong and fierce and he liked to eat people – most of all young ones! Theseus was not only brave, but brainy too.

He went into the Labyrinth with a ball of string, which he let out as he walked so that he would be able to find his way back. Then he attacked the Minotaur and killed it.

I was thinking about that in the museum, because one of the first things we saw was a pot with a picture on it of Theseus fighting the Queen of the *Amazons*. The Amazons were women fighters.

The Greeks liked pots. There were lots in the museum. Some were painted with pictures of myths, gods, or Greek daily life. On some pots, the pictures were in black. This is called Black Figure pottery. On others, the figures were red. This is called Red Figure pottery. The Greeks used the pots to keep things like water, wine and olive oil. Some of them were so big you could have kept a child in them!

"You can write about those pots in your project," Mum said.

"Yes," I said. *But pots are not very exciting*, I thought.

I liked the sculptures more. Some of them were made of stone, others were made of marble. Lots of them were of gods and goddesses. I saw one of Nike with wings.

I asked her to bring me victory and help me win the Troy Trophy.

Quite a few of the sculptures had no head, so you had to guess what they must have looked like. The one I liked best was a girl. She was holding a bird in her left hand and a fold of her dress in her right hand. But who was she? Was she just a human girl or was she a goddess? What was her story? I decided it was going to be part of my project to find out.

My top five monster stats

1. The *Stymphalian* birds had beaks, claws and feathers made of bronze and they could throw their feathers like arrows and kill anyone who came near. The Greek hero *Heracles* (or *Hercules* as the Romans called him) had to kill them for one of his twelve labours (the 12 almost impossible tasks he had been set to do by the gods).

2. The *Chimera* was a fire-breathing beast with a lion's head, a goat's body and a snake for a tail! It was killed by the hero *Bellerophon* (riding the winged horse *Pegasus*), who shot metal arrow-heads into its mouth. The metal melted in the flames of its breath and burnt its insides out.

3. If you cut off one of the nine heads of the snake-like monster *Hydra*, it would grow another one. And it could kill you just by breathing on you.

4. The *Sphinx* was half-woman, half-lion with the wings of an eagle and it used to ask travellers this riddle: "What has four legs in the morning, two in the afternoon, and three in the evening?" If they got it wrong, she ate them! (The answer is man: first he is a baby who crawls, then an adult standing up, and then he is old and has a stick to help him walk.)

5. The mother of all monsters is *Echidna*. She had a beautiful woman's face but a snake's body and she ate men raw.

Her children included Cerberus (the
three-headed dog), the Sphinx, the
Chimera and the Hydra. (I would not like
to have been in their house at dinner
time!)

Chapter 4
Birds

I worked hard on my Ancient Greek project at home and at school. Mrs Moody-Brown said she was very pleased with what I had done.

"There's lots of good information and some lovely drawing, Arnold," she said. "But your writing could be neater."

"Greeks wrote with pens made from reeds," I said, "and they used ink made from water, gum and soot. They didn't have paper either, like us. They wrote on *papyrus*. It was made from the long stems of the papyrus plant which were pressed and stuck together."

"And they still wrote more neatly than you, Arnold," Mrs Moody-Brown sighed. But then she smiled. "Keep up the good work," she said.

I loved learning facts about Ancient Greece. Every day I would tell my mum something new that I had learned. I told my sister Ellie too. She was not very impressed. She said she would even rather hear facts about football than Ancient Greece. "Arnie," she said with a yawn, "you are boring me – and that *is* a fact."

I could have told her that if she was living in Ancient Greece then, even at 13, she probably would have been married and that really would have been boring. But I decided to keep that fact to myself.

I clicked on some websites for information about the Ancient Greeks and birds to see if I could learn more about the headless girl in the museum. I found out that the Ancient Greeks did keep birds as pets, but not in cages, and they used pigeons to send messages.

I learned about some famous birds from Greek myths. The *Phoenix* was a bird who set fire to itself at the end of its life and then a new Phoenix rose from its ashes. The *Griffon* had the body of a lion but the head of an eagle. Then there were the *Harpies*, who were noisy, nasty, dirty beasts with wings and the claws and body of a vulture, but the head of an ugly old woman. They used to torment people – like Steven Morris tormented me.

There was a sad bird myth too about a woman called *Alycone* whose husband drowned. When she waded out into the sea to get his body the gods took pity on her and turned them both into beautiful blue-green birds called *halcyons*, which are like kingfishers.

Many of the top Greek gods and goddesses who lived on Mount Olympus had their own special bird. *Hera*, the wife of the king god *Zeus*, liked the peacock. The vulture was the bird of *Ares*, the god of war. The crow was the bird of the sun god *Apollo*. I didn't think that my girl was any of these gods, but was she a priestess perhaps who served one of them? Or was she someone from a myth? One thing was for sure - she was very *myth*sterious!

Well, maybe I would have to make up my own myth about her ...

My top five Gods and Goddesses stats

1. When the god of fire *Hephaestus* was born, his mother Hera thought he was so ugly she threw him off Mount Olympus!

He got his own back by sending her a throne that she could not get up from once she had sat down. He also made bronze tripods that could move on their own, and robot watchdogs!

2. The god of the underworld, *Hades*, had a helmet that made him invisible. People were scared of him and didn't like to say his name so they called him "the invisible one."

3. The goddess of magic and witchcraft was *Hecate*. Her followers left food for her at crossroads: fish, cakes with lit candles and dead puppies!

4. The goddess **Athena** was the daughter of the chief god **Zeus**, but she didn't have a mother. She sprang fully grown and wearing armour from her dad's head. One of the most famous buildings in the world, the Parthenon in Athens, was built as a temple to Athena. Inside there was a statue of her that was 13 metres high!

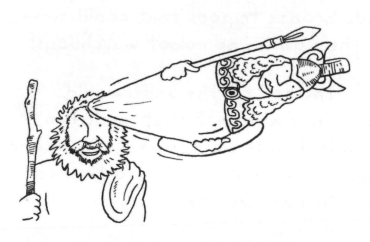

5. The god of the sea, Poseidon, was so strong and violent that when he threw his trident (a huge fork with 3 prongs) into the ground it caused an earthquake!

Chapter 5
Facts and Fiction

There was only one week to go before the open day when our Greek projects would be put on display and Dr Troy Smith would choose the winner.

"I think your project is the best, Stat Man," said Thomas Jones. "Your stats are cool."

"Thanks," I said. Katie Lee said she thought that Miranda Best would win. Miranda Best was top of the class. She won all the prizes. I saw her project. It looked very neat. But was it the best?

Thomas Jones said that it was going to be a battle between the two of us – "Arnie versus Miranda, boy against girl," he said. Thomas Jones loved battles.

"I don't think I am very good at battles," I said.

"Don't worry, Stat Man," Thomas said. "Think like a Spartan. They didn't care how big the army was against them. They knew they would win."

"They didn't win at the battle of *Thermopylae*," I said.

"Well, they would have done," Thomas Jones said, "if the other side hadn't cheated."

I kept on working on my project. My mum said she had never seen me work so hard. She said I was working like a slave. I told her that there were probably as many slaves as free people in Ancient Greece, and they did most of the jobs around the house, like cooking and cleaning.

"Sounds like I'm the slave then," Mum joked.

I showed Dad my project.

"What do you think?" I asked.

"Well, Arnie, it's all Greek to me," he said. Then he laughed. I frowned at him. "It's a joke," he said. "You say 'It's all Greek to me' when you don't understand something."

"Oh," I muttered. Sometimes my dad is all Greek to me.

I still hadn't solved the mystery of the bird girl. I had a picture of her from the museum that I wanted to put in my project. I could just put it in with "A Greek sculpture" underneath, but that seemed boring. She was my favourite thing in the museum, after all. I needed to think of something better.

I thought the bird could be a swallow. The Ancient Greeks liked swallows. I liked swallows too. There was a nest of them in an old barn at the back of our house last summer. There was a Greek story about a girl called *Philomela*. She had her tongue cut out by the wicked husband of her sister. The gods turned her into a swallow, and they turned her sister *Procne* into a nightingale. It was not a nice story. I decided to make my own story up – my myth about Philomela.

Making up stories is not easy. I had to think very hard. But in the end I did it. This is the story I made up.

Once there was a girl called Philomela. She was very kind and beautiful. She loved all animals, but best of all she loved birds. Her favourite bird was a swallow. She liked the way it flew and she liked to hear it sing because then she knew that spring had come. The birds loved Philomela because she fed them and looked after them. Once she found a swallow shivering in the snow and she wrapped it in the folds of her dress to make it warm again.

One day a king saw Philomela and fell in love with her beauty. He wanted to marry her. But Philomela did not want to marry the king because he was a cruel man. He liked to hunt animals and birds with his hawks. So Philomela said she would not marry the king. The king got very angry. He said that if she did not marry him then he would kill her. Philomela asked the gods for help.

They took pity on her because she was such a kind and good person. Just as the cruel king was about to kill her, the gods turned her into a swallow so that she could be with all her bird friends and she lived happily ever after. As for the cruel king, he was killed in a battle and eaten by his own hawks.

There. That was it. At last, my project
was finished.

My top Greek battle stats

1. In 490 B.C. the men of Athens (the Athenians) faced the Persians in an important battle at Marathon. The Athenians sent a runner to Sparta to get help, but the Spartans said they couldn't do anything until after the full moon - and by the time they turned up, the battle was over! The Athenians won and the same runner ran to Athens with the news. He died from the effort. But the Olympic marathon is run in his memory.

2. Before a battle, mothers in Sparta said to their sons: "Come back with your shield in your hand or come back carried on top of it." (That meant dead!) If you came back without your shield, that meant you had dropped it so you could run away

faster. You would then be called a "Trembler" (a coward). You were forced to wear silly clothes and grow a moustache on one side of your face!

3. At the battle of Thermopylae in 480 B.C., 300 Spartans held up the whole Persian army of **10,000** soldiers called the "Immortals" for a week. In the end a Spartan betrayed his own army and all **300** of them were killed.

4. Alexander the Great always rode into battle on his horse Bucephalus, which he himself had tamed as a boy. When the horse died in June 326 B.C., in India after Alexander's last great battle, the king named a city after him.

5. In 212 B.C. in the city of Syracuse, the inventor Archimedes came up with a brilliant plan to destroy the Roman fleet. He got the Greek soldiers to polish their shields. Then he asked them to stand in a curve and use their shields as mirrors to reflect the sun's rays at the Roman ships, and set them on fire.

Chapter 6
And the Winner is ...

I had butterflies in my tummy when I went to school that morning. It was like when I played for my football team Lime Green Rovers in the Cup Final. I was very nervous. My hands were shaking when I gave my project to Mrs Moody-Brown.

She smiled. "I want you to know, Arnold, that I'm very proud of you," she said.

"I don't know who's going to win, but you've worked really hard. Well done."

"Thank you, Miss," I said.

Dr Troy Smith arrived soon after. He was wearing jeans and red trainers like before but he had a different T-shirt. It had a picture of a man's face on it. He had a small flat nose and a very big beard. Under the picture were the words, "All I know is I know nothing".

I put my hand up. "Excuse me, Dr Troy Smith, is that an Ancient Greek on your T-shirt?"

Dr Troy Smith nodded. "It is," he said. "It is a picture of a great Greek philosopher called *Socrates*."

"What's a flossofur?" Katie Lee asked.

"It's someone who thinks a lot about life," said Dr Troy Smith.

"Are you a philosopher?" Thomas Jones asked.

"A bit," said Dr Troy Smith, "but not like Socrates. Thinking about life was his job and he tried to make other people think about their lives too and why they did what they did. One of the things he said was 'All I know is I know nothing'. I think he means that there is always more to know and you should never stop learning. I think that's a very important lesson for all of us."

"Hear, hear," said Mrs Moody-Brown.

"And I'm going to need some of Socrates' wisdom now, because I've got to judge your projects," said Dr Troy Smith.

My tummy was suddenly all full of butterflies again.

"It'll be a very hard task," said Mrs Moody-Brown.

"I'm sure it will," said Dr Troy Smith.

It took Dr Troy Smith the whole morning to read all our projects. The whole class was very excited. We could not keep our minds on our work. Who was going to win the Troy Trophy? If only it could be me …

At last, after lunch and when the register was done, Dr Troy Smith came back into our class. He was holding a silver trophy, which was in the shape of a man throwing a discus, as if he were an athlete in the Olympic Games. *That must be the Troy Trophy*, I thought.

Dr Troy Smith smiled at us all. "I really enjoyed reading your projects," he said.

"They are full of interesting facts and wonderful pictures. I hope you had as much fun doing them as I had looking at them. That's the best morning I've spent for a long time." He looked at the trophy again. "Now in a competition there has to be a winner. It's been very, very hard but I've decided that the first winner of the Troy Trophy should be ..."

Please let it be me, please let it be me, I begged silently. The butterflies in my tummy were fluttering so much I felt sick.

"... Miranda Best," said Dr Troy Smith.

The girls all cheered. Some of the boys groaned, but most of them cheered too, because most people liked Miranda Best. She always won but she never boasted.

Her face was a huge grin as she went up to collect the Troy Trophy and the book-

token from Dr Troy Smith. Everyone
clapped. Mrs Moody-Brown took a photo.

We thought that was the end but it
wasn't.

"Now, I gave Miranda the prize because she had done some very good research for her project. It had beautiful pictures and was very well-presented," said Dr Troy Smith. "But I've decided to give another prize. This person's work was not nearly as neat or well presented, but it was packed with brilliant facts and, best of all, it had imagination. This person even made up his own myth. In fact he reminds me a bit of me when I was at this school."

Dr Troy Smith was smiling at me and my heart was beating as if there was a bird inside flapping its wings.

"So I'm giving this prize to Arnold," said Dr Troy Smith.

I got out of my seat and everyone . cheered and shouted and someone did a wolf-whistle. I think I was smiling even more than Miranda Best. "Well done, Stat Man!"

said Dr Troy Smith and he gave me a bronze metal statue of a man with a *lyre*, which is a sort of harp. Then he shook my hand. *I'm never going to wash my hand again*, I thought. Mrs Moody-Brown took a photo. Everyone cheered and clapped again.

That photo is now on my wall next to my Lime Green Rovers Cup Final Stat Sheet. I look at it every night – and my bronze statue too.

One day, I, Arnold James Kean – alias Arnie and Stat Man – am going to be a famous museum curator, just like Dr Troy Smith!

My top five famous Greeks stats

1. Alexander the Great was one of the greatest generals ever and was never beaten in battle. He conquered most of Asia. He became king of Greece in 334 B.C. and was only 32 when he died in 323 B.C.

2. The writer Aesop was a slave who lived in the 6th century B.C. His stories (called fables) are some of the most famous in the world: 'The Tortoise and the Hare', 'The Boy Who Cried Wolf', 'The Fox and the Crow'. They all have morals at the end. But Aesop upset some priests at a place called *Delphi* and they threw him off a cliff top. I wonder what the moral of that is!

3. Archimedes was a great thinker. Once, when he was in the bath he made a brilliant discovery. He jumped out

and ran naked into the streets shouting, "Eureka! Eureka!" (I've found it! I've found it!)

4. Draco was a very cruel ruler of Athens. In 621 B.C. he made it a law that people should be put to death for even small crimes - like stealing a cabbage or being lazy - as well as big ones! He said it wasn't right that big and little crimes got punished in the same way, but he couldn't think up anything worse than death!

5. The Ancient Greeks loved going to the theatre to see funny plays (comedies) and sad plays (tragedies). One of the most famous writers of tragedies was a man called Aeschylus. His death was very strange. In 450 B.C. he was killed when an eagle mistook his bald head for a stone and dropped a tortoise on it! (Was that a comic or tragic end? I will let you make up your own mind!)

AUTHOR FACT FILE
ALAN DURANT

If you could invent a new sport for the Olympic Games what would it be?
Bogey flicking.

If you could be any Greek monster or god – who would you be and why?
Hermes. Those winged sandals are cool.

Which monster or god would you least like to be?
Atlas. Well, how would you like to be named after a boring book of maps?

What evil things would you hide away in Pandora's box?
Stewed apple and my son's pants.

If you could be a god for the day, what would you use your powers to do?
I'd make my children tidy and make sausages grow on trees.

ILLUSTRATOR FACT FILE
BRETT HUDSON

If you could invent a new sport for the Olympic Games what would it be?
The 100m hurdles for all the Olympic mascots past and present, or fencing on horseback.

What evil things would you hide away in Pandora's box?
People who are arrogant and semolina, which I think is horrible.

If you could shave a secret message onto someone's head, what would you write and who would you send it to?
"Don't forget it's my birthday on Feb 16th". I'd send it to my friends and family the week before.

If you could be any Greek monster or god – who would you be and why?
The minotaur because he was big and powerful but I don't like the idea of living in a dark maze all the time.

Barrington Stoke would like to thank all its readers for commenting on the manuscript before publication and in particular:

Thomas Clarke

Annabel Collier

Matthew Dowse

Eilidh Johnston

James McCaffery

Duncan Menzies

Become a Consultant!

Would you like to give us feedback on our titles before they are published? Contact us at the email address below – we'd love to hear from you!

info@barringtonstoke.co.uk
www.barringtonstoke.co.uk

Try another book in the "fyi" series!
Fiction with stacks of facts

The Egyptians
The Three-Legged Mummy by Viv French

Boxing
The Greatest by Alan Gibbons

Rock Music
Diary Of A Trainee Rock God
by Jonathan Meres

Surveillance
The Doomsday Watchers
by Steve Barlow and Steve Skidmore

All available from our website:
www.barringtonstoke.co.uk